A Good Samaritan

by

Mary Raymond Shipman Andrews

A GOOD SAMARITAN

The little District Telegraph boy, with a dirty face, stood at the edge of the desk, and, rubbing his sleeve across his cheek, made it unnecessarily dirtier.

"Answer, sir?"

"No—yes—wait a minute." Reed tore the yellow envelope and spread the telegram. It read:

"Do I meet you at your office or at Martin's and what time?"

"The devil!" Reed commented, and the boy blinked indifferently. He was used to stronger. "The casual Rex all over! Yes, boy, there's an answer." He scribbled rapidly, and the two lines of writing said this:

"Waiting for you at office now. Hurry up. C. Reed."

He fumbled in his pocket and gave the youngster a coin. "See that it's sent instantly—like lightning. Run!" and the sharp little son of New York was off before the last word was well out.

Half an hour later, to Reed waiting at his office in Broadway impatiently, there strolled in a good-looking and leisurely young man with black clothes on his back and peace and good-will on his face. "Hope I haven't kept you waiting, Carty," he remarked in friendly tones. "Plenty of time, isn't there?"

"No, there isn't," his cousin answered, and there was a touch of snap in the accent. "Really, Rex, you ought to grow up and be responsible. It was distinctly arranged that you should call here for me at six, and now it's a quarter before seven."

"Couldn't remember the hour or the place to save my life," the younger man asserted earnestly. "I'm just as sorry as I can be, Carty. You see I did remember we were to dine at Martin's. So much I got all right—and that was something, wasn't it, Carty?" he inquired with an air of wistful pride, and the frown on the face of the other dissolved in laughter.

"Rex, there's no making you over—worse luck. Come along. I've got to go home to dress after dinner you see, before we make our call. You'll do, on the strength of being a theological student."

The situation was this: Reginald Fairfax, in his last year at the Theological Seminary, in this month of May, and lately ordained, had been seriously spoken of as assistant to the Rector of the great church of St. Eric's. It was a remarkable position to come the way of an undergraduate, and his brilliant record at the seminary was one of the two things which made it possible. The other was the friendship and interest of his cousin, Carter Reed, head clerk in the law firm of Rush, Walden, Lee and Lee, whose leading member, Judge Rush, was also senior warden at St. Eric's. Reed had called Judge Rush's attention to his young cousin's career, and, after some inquiry, the vestryman had asked that the young man should be brought to see him, to discuss certain questions bearing on the work. It was almost equivalent to a call coming from such a man, and Reed was delighted; but here his troubles began. In vain did he hopefully fix date after date with the slippery Rex— something always interfered. Twice, to his knowledge, it had been the chance of seeing a girl from Orange which had thrown over the chance of seeing the man of influence and power. Once the evening had been definitely arranged with Judge Rush himself, and Reed was obliged to go alone and report that the candidate had disappeared into a tenement district and no one knew where to find him. The effect of that was fortunately good —Judge Rush was rather pleased than otherwise that a young clergyman should be so taken up with his work as to forget his interests. But Reed was most anxious that this evening's appointment should go off successfully, while Rex was as light-hearted as a bird. Any one would have thought it was Reed's own future he was laboring over instead of that of the youngster who had a gift of making men care for him and work for him without effort on his own part.

The two walked down Broadway toward the elevated road, Rex's dark eyes gathering amusement here and there in the crowded way as they went.

"Look at Billy Strong—why there's Billy Strong across the street. Come over and I'll present you, Carty. Just the chap you want to meet. He's a great athlete—on the water-polo team of the New York Athletic Club, you know —as much of an old sport as you are." And Reed found himself swung across and standing before a powerful, big figure of a man, almost before he could answer. There was another man with the distinguished Billy, and Reed had not regarded the two for more than one second before he discovered that they were both in a distinct state of intoxication. In fact, Strong proclaimed the truth at once, false shame cast to the winds. He threw his arm about Rex's neck with a force of affection which almost knocked down the quartette.

"Recky," he bubbled, "good old Recky—bes' fren' ev' had"

"Recky," he bubbled, "good old Recky—bes' fren' ev' had—I'm drunk, Recky—too bad. We're both drunk. Take's home." Rex glanced at his cousin in dismay, and Strong repeated his invitation cordially. "Take's home, Recky," he insisted, with the easy air of a man who confers an honor. "'S up to you, Recky."

Rex looked at his frowning cousin doubtfully, pleadingly.

"It almost seems as if it was, doesn't it, Carty?" he said. "We can't leave them like this."

"I don't see why we can't—I can," Reed asserted. "It's none of our business, Rex, and we really haven't time to palaver. Come along."

The gentle soul of Rex Fairfax was surprisingly firm. "Carty, they'd be arrested in five minutes," he reasoned. "It's a wonder they haven't been already. And Billy's people—it would break their hearts. I know some of them well, you see. I was with him only last week over in Orange."

"Oh!" Reed groaned. "That Girl from Orange again." He opened his lips once more to launch nervous English against this quixotism, but Strong interposed.

"'S all true," he solemnly stated, fixing his eyes rollingly on Reed. "Got Orange-colored cousin what break Recky's heart if don't take's home. Y'see—y'see—" The President of these United States in a cabinet council would have stopped to listen to him, so freighted with great facts coming was his confidential manner. "Y'see—wouldn't tell ev'body—only you," and he laid a mighty hand on Reed's shoulder. "I'm so drunk. Awful pity—too bad," and he sighed deeply. "Now, Recky, ol' man, take's home."

"Who's your friend, Billy?"

"Who's your friend, Billy?" Rex inquired, disregarding this appeal.

Billy burst into a shout of laughter which Fairfax promptly clipped by putting his hand over the big man's mouth. "He's bes' joke yet," Strong remarked through Rex's fingers. "He's go'n' kill himself," and he kissed the restraining hand gallantly.

The two sober citizens turned and stared at the gentlemen. He looked it. He looked as if there could be no step deeper into the gloom which enveloped him, except suicide. He nodded darkly as the two regarded him.

"Uh-huh. Life's failure. Lost cuff-button. Won't live to be indecent. Go'n' kill m'self soon's this dizhiness goesh pasht. Billy's drunk, but I'm subject to —to dizhiness."

Rex turned to his cousin with a gesture. "You see, Carty, we can't leave them. I'm just as disappointed as you are, but it would be a beastly thing to do, to let them get pulled in as common drunks. What's your friend's name?" he demanded again of Strong.

"Got lovely name," he averred eagerly. "Good ol' moth-eaten name. Name's Schuyler VanCourtlandt Van de Water—ain't it Schuylie—ain't that your name—or's that mine? I—I f'rget lil' things," he said in an explanatory manner.

But the suicide spoke up for himself. "Tha's my name," he said aggressively. "Knew it in a minute. Tha's my father's name and my grandfath's name, and my great grandfath's name and my great-great——"

"Stop," said Rex tersely, and the man stopped. "Now tell me where you live."

Billy Strong leaned over and punched the man in the ribs. "You lemme tell 'em. Lives nine-thous-n sixt'-four East West Street," he addressed Rex, and chuckled.

"Don't be a donkey, Billy—tell me his right address." Rex spoke with annoyance—this scene was getting tiresome, and although Reed was laughing hopelessly, he was on his mind.

"Oh! F'got!" Billy's tipsy coyness was elephantine. "Lives *six* thous'n *sev*'nty four North S—South Street," and he roared with laughter.

Rex was about to learn how to manage Billy Strong. "Bill," he said, "be decent. You're making me lots of trouble," and Billy burst into tears and sobbed out:

"Wouldn' make Recky trouble for worlds—good ol' Recky—half-witted ol' goat, but bes' fren' ev' had," and the address was captured.

Rex turned to his cousin, his winning, deprecating manner warning Reed but softening him against his will. "Carty," he said, "there's nothing for it, but for you to take one chap and I the other and see 'em home. It's only a little after seven and we ought to be able to meet by half-past eight—at the Hotel Netherland, say—that's near the Rush's. We'll have to give up dinner, but we'll get a sandwich somewhere, and we'll do. I'll take Strong because he's more troublesome—I think I can manage him. It's awfully good of you, and I can tell you I appreciate it. But it wouldn't be civilized to do less, old Carty, would it?" And Reed found himself, grumbling but docile, linked to the suicide's arm, and guiding his shuffling foot-steps in the way they should go.

"Now, we'll both kill ourselves, old Carty, won't we?" Rex heard his cousin's charge mumble cheerfully as they started off, with a visible lengthening of his gloom at the thought of companionship at death.

Strong was marching along with an unearthly decorum that should have made Fairfax suspicious. But instead it cheered his optimistic soul immensely. "Good for you old man," he said encouragingly. "At this rate we'll get you home in no time." And Billy, at that second, thrust out his great shoulder into the crowd, and almost knocked a man down. The man, whirled sidewise in front of them, glared savagely.

"What do you mean by that?" he demanded. Strong, to whom nothing would have given more joy than a tussle, bent down and peered into the other's face.

"Is it a man or a monkey?" he piped, and shrieked with laughter.

The man's strained temper broke suddenly and Rex caught him by the arm as he was about to spring for Strong, and promptly threw himself between the two.

"Look here, Billy," he remonstrated, "if you fight anybody it's got to be me," and he spoke over his shoulder to the stranger. "You see what I'm up against. I'm getting him home—do just go on," and the man went.

But Billy's head was in his guardian's neck and he was spluttering and sobbing. "Fight you? Nev'—s' help me—nev'—Fight poor, ole fool Recky—bes' fren' ev' had? No sir. I wouldn' fight you Recky," and he raised a tear-stained face and gazed mournfully into his eyes. "D'ye think I'd——"

"Oh, shut up!" Rex ejaculated, "and hold your head up, Billy. You make me sick."

The intoxicated heavy freight being under way again, Rex looked about for the rest of the train, but in vain. After a halt of a minute or so he decided that they were lost and would have to stay lost, the situation being too precarious, in this land of policemen, with one hundred and ninety pounds of noisy uncertainty on his hands, to risk any unnecessary movement. Billy kept every breath of time alive and varied. Within two minutes of the first adventure he managed to put his elbow clearly and forcibly into a small man's mouth, and before the other could resent it:

"'S my elbow, sir," he said, haughtily, stopping and staring down.

"Well, why in thunder don't you keep it where it belongs?" snapped the man, and Billy caught him by the sleeve.

"Lil' sir," he said impressively, "if you should bite off my elbow, you saucy baggage"—and the thought was too much for him. Tears filling his eyes he turned to Rex. "Recky, you spank that lil' sir," he pleaded brokenly. "He's too lil' for me—I'd hurt him"—and Rex meditated again. A shock came when they reached the corner of Broadway and Chambers Street. "Up's' daisy," crowed Billy Strong, and swung Fairfax facing uptown with a mighty heave.

"The Elevated station's down a block, old chap," explained the sober contingent. "We have to take the Elevated to Seventy-second you know, and walk across to your place."

Billy looked at him pityingly. "You poor lil' pup," he crooned. "Didn' I keep tellin' you had to go Chris'pher Street ferry meet a girl? Goin' theater with girl." He tipped his derby one-sided and started off on a cakewalk.

Rex had to march beside him willy-nilly. "Look here, Billy," he reasoned, exasperated at this entirely fresh twist in the corkscrew business of getting Strong home. "Look here, Billy, this is tommy-rot. You haven't any date with a girl, and if you had you couldn't keep it. Come along home, man; that's the place for you."

But Billy was suddenly a Gibraltar of firmness. "Got date with lovely blue-eyed girlie—couldn't dish'point her. Unmanly deed—Recky, d' *you* want bes' fren' ev' had to do unmanly deed, and dish'point trustin' female? Nev', Recky—nev', ol' man. Lesh be true to th' ladies till hell runs dry—Oh, 'scuse me Recky—f'got you was parson—till *well* runs dry, meant say. That all right? Come on t' Chris'pher Street." And in spite of desperate attempts, of long argument and appeal on Rex's part, to Christopher Street they went.

The ministering angel had no hankering to risk his charge in a street-car, so, as the distance was not great, they walked.

Fairfax's dread was that, having saved his friend so far, he should attract the attention of a policeman and be arrested. So he kept a sharp lookout for bluecoats and passed them studiously on the other side. What was his horror therefore, turning a corner, to turn squarely into the majestic arm of the law, and what was his greater horror, to hear Billy Strong suavely address him. Billy lifted his hat to the large, fat officer as he might have lifted it to his sweetheart in her box at the Horse Show.

"Would you have the g—goodness to tell me," he inquired, with distinguished courtesy, "if this is"—Billy's articulation was improving, but otherwise he was just as tipsy as ever—"if this is—Chris-to-pher Street—or —or Wednesday?"

"Hey?" inquired the policeman, and stared. Repartee seemed not to be his forte.

"Thank you—thank you very much—very, very much—old rhinoceros"

"Thank you—thank you very much"—Billy's gratitude spilled over conventional limits—"very, *very* much—old rhinoceros," he finished, and shot suddenly ahead, dragging Rex with him into the whirlpool of a moving crowd, and it dawned on the policeman five minutes later that the courtly gentleman was drunk.

The anxiety of this game was its unexpectedness. Strong, in the turn of a hand grew playful, after the fashion of a mammoth kitten. He bounded this way and that, knocking into somebody inevitably at every leap, and at each contact he wheeled toward the injured and lifted his hat and bowed low and brought out "I—beg—your—pardon" with a drawl of sarcastic emphasis too insulting to be described.

"Billy," pleaded Rex, taking to pathos, "don't do that again. You'll get arrested, and maybe they'll arrest me too, and you don't want to get me into a hole, do you?"

Billy stopped short with a suddenness which came near to upsetting his guide, and put both large hands on Rex's shoulders, and gazed into his eyes with a world of blurred affection. "Reck, ol'fel'," and his voice broke with a sob, "if I got you into hole, I'd jump in hole after you, and I'd—and I'd— pull hole in after both of us, and then I'd—I'd tell hole you was bes' fren' ev' had, and——"

"Come along and behave," cut in the victim of this devotion shortly. "Don't be a fool."

Strong lifted a fatherly forefinger. "Naughty naughty! Shouldn' call brother fool. Danger hell fire if you call brother fool. Nev' min', Recky—we un'stand each other. Two fools. I'm go'n behave." He knocked his derby in the back so it rested on his nose, stuck his chin up to meet it, and started off in the most unmistakable semblance of a tipsy man to be met anywhere. "See me behavin'?" he remarked sidewise, with a gleam of rollicking deviltry out of his eyes.

"So tired" he remarked. "Go'n have good nap now"

Christopher Street ferry was reached safely by a miracle, and inside the ferry-house Strong made a bee line for a truck and threw his great body full length upon it with a loud yawn of joy. "So tired," he remarked. "Go'n have good nap now," and he closed his eyes peacefully.

"See here, Billy, this won't do. You said you had to meet a girl—what about that?"

"Oh, tha's all right," Billy agreed easily. "You meet girl—tell her you got me drunk," and he turned over and prepared for slumber. Strenuous argument was necessary to rouse him even to half a sense of responsibility. "Recky, dear, you—'noy me," he said with severity, coming to a sitting position and contemplating Rex with mild displeasure. "What kin' girl? Why, jes' girly-girl. Lovely blue-eyed girly-girl—kind of girl—colored hair,"—he swept his hand descriptively over his own black locks. "Wears sort of—skirts, you know—you 'member the kind. All of 'em same thing— well, she wears 'em too. Tha's all," and he dropped heavily back to the truck and retired into his coat collar.

Rex shook him. "That won't do, Billy. I can't pick out a girl on that. Will there be a chaperone with her?"

"No!" thundered Billy.

"How is a girl allowed to go to the theater with you without a chaperone?" inquired Rex incredulously. "This is New York."

Strong brought down his fist. "Death to chaperones! *A bas les chaperones!* Don't you think girl's mother trust her to me? Look at me! I'll be chaperone to tha' girl, and father, 'n' mother, 'n' a few uncles and aunts." He threw his arm out with a gesture which comprised the universe. "I'll be all the world to tha' girl. You go meet her 'n' tell her you got me drunk," he concluded with a radiant smile.

Rex considered. There seemed to be enough method in Strong's madness to justify the belief that he had an engagement. If so, he must by all means wait and trust to luck to pick out the "lovely blue-eyed girlie" who was the "party of the other part," and hope for an inspiration as to what to tell her. She might be with or without a chaperone, she might be any variety of the species, but Strong seemed to be quite clear that she had blue eyes.

The crowd from the incoming boat began to unload into the ferry-house, and Rex placed himself anxiously by the entrance. Three or four thin men scurried in advance, then a bunch of stout and middle-aged persons straggled along puffing. Then came a set of young people in theater array, chattering and laughing as they hurried, and another set, and another—the main body of the little army was upon him. Rex scanned them for a girl alone or a girl with her mother. Ah! here she was—this must be Strong's "blue-eyed girlie." She was alone and pretty, a little under-bred and blond. Rex lifted his hat.

"I beg your pardon," he said, in his most winning way; "are you waiting for Mr. Strong?"

The girl threw up her head and looked frightened, and then angry.

"No, I am not," she said, and then, with a haughty look, "I call you pretty saucy," and Rex was left mortified and silent, while a passing man murmured, "Served you right," and a woman laughed scornfully. He stalked across to the tranquil form on the truck.

"Billy," he said, and shook a massive shoulder. "Wake up. Tell me that girl's name."

Strong opened his eyes like a baby waked from dewy sleep. "Wha's that, Recky—dear old Recky—bes' fren'——"

"Cut that out," said Rex, sharply. "Tell me the name of the girl you're waiting here to meet," and he laughed a short bitter laugh. The girl whom "Billy" was waiting to meet! Rex was getting tired and hungry.

Strong smiled a gentle, obstinate, tipsy smile and shook his head. "No, Recky, dear ol' fren'—bes' fren'—well, nev' min'. Can't tell girl's name; tha's her secret."

"Don't be an ass, Billy—quick, now, tell me the name."

"Naughty, naughty!" quoted Billy again, and waggled his forefinger. "Danger hell fire! Couldn' tell girl's name, Recky—be dishon'able. Couldn', no, couldn'. Anythin' else—ask m' anythin' else in all these wide worlds"— and he struck his breast with fervor. "Tell you *anythin'*, Recky, but couldn' betray trustin' girl's secret."

"Billy, can't you give me an idea what the girl's like?" pleaded Rex desperately. Billy smiled up at him drowsily. "Perfectly good girl," he elucidated. "Good eyes, good wind, kind to mother—perfectly good girl in ev—every r-respect," he concluded, emphasizing his sentences by articulating them. He dropped his chin into his chest with a recumbent bow, and his arm described an impressive semicircle. "Present to her 'surances my most disting'shed consider-ration—soon's you find her," and he went flop on his side and was asleep.

Rex had to give it up. He heard the gates rattling open for the next boat-load, and took his stand again, bracing himself for another rebuff. The usual vanguard, the usual quicksilver bunch of humanity, massing, separating, flowing this way and that, and in the midst of them a fair-haired, timid-looking young girl, walking quietly with down-cast eyes, as if unused to being in big New York alone at eight o'clock at night. Rex stood in front of her with bared head.

"I beg your pardon," he repeated his formula; "are you looking for Mr. Strong?"

The startled eyes lifted to his a short second, then dropped again. "No, for Mr. Week," she answered softly, and unconscious of witticism, melted into the throng.

This was a heavy boat-load, for it was just theater time—they were still coming. And suddenly his heart bounded and stopped. Of course—he was utterly foolish not to have known—it was she—Billy Strong's bewitching cousin, the girl from Orange. There she stood with her big, brown eyes searching, gazing here and there, as lovely, as incongruous as a wood-nymph strayed into a political meeting. The feather of her hat tossed in the May breeze; the fading light from the window behind her shone through loose hair about her face, turned it into a soft dark aureole; the gray of her tailor gown was crisp and fresh as spring-time. To Rex's eyes no picture had ever been more satisfying.

Suddenly she caught sight of him, and her face lighted as if lamps had shone out of a twilight, and in a second he had her hand in his, and was talking away, with responsibility and worry, and that heavy weight on the truck back there, quite gone out of the world. She was in it, and himself—the world was full. The girl seemed to be as oblivious of outside facts, as he, for it was quite two minutes, and the last straggler from the boat had disappeared into the street before she broke into one of his sentences.

"Why, but—I forgot. You made me forget entirely, Mr. Fairfax. I'm going to the theater with my cousin, Billy Strong. He ought to be here—where is he?"

Rex shivered lest her roving eyes might answer the question, for Billy's truck with Billy slumbering peacefully on it, lay in full view not fifty feet away. But her gaze passed unsuspiciously over the prostrate, huddled form.

"It's very queer—I'm sure this was the right boat." She looked up at his face anxiously, and he almost moaned aloud. What was he going to say to her?

"That's what I'm here for, Miss Margery—to explain about Billy. He—he isn't feeling at all himself to-night, and it's utterly impossible for him to go with you." To his astonishment her face broke into a very satisfied smile. "Oh—well, I'm sorry Billy's ill, but we'll hope for the best, and I won't really object to you as a substitute, you know. Of course it's improper, and mother wouldn't think of letting me go with you—but I'm going. Mother won't mind when I tell her it's done. I've never been alone with a man to anything, except with my cousin—it's like stealing watermelons, isn't it? Don't you think it's rather fun?"

Staggered by the situation, Fairfax thought desperately and murmured something which sounded like "Oochee-Goochee," as he tried to recall it later. The girl's gay voice went on: "It would be wicked to waste the tickets. City people aren't going to the theater as late as this, so we won't see any one we know. I think it's a dispensation of Providence, and I'd be a poor-spirited mouse to waste the chance. I think I'll go with you—don't you?"

"Could he—couldn't he?"

Could he leave that prostrate form on the truck and snatch at this bit of heaven dangling before him? Could he—Couldn't he? No, he could not. It would be a question of fifteen minutes perhaps before the drowsy Billy would be marching to the police station, and in his entirely casual and fearless state of mind, the big athlete would make history for some policeman, his friend could not doubt, before he got there. Rex had put his hand to this intoxicated plow and he must not look back, even when the prospect backwards was so bewilderingly attractive, so tantalizingly easy. He stammered badly when, at length, the silence which followed the soft voice had to be filled.

"I'm simply—simply—broken up, Miss Margery," and the girl's eyes looked at him with a sweet wideness that made it harder. "I don't know how to tell you, and I don't know how to resign myself to it either, but I—I can't take you to the theater. I—I've got to—got to—well, you see, I've got to be with Billy."

She spoke quickly at that. "Mr. Fairfax, is Billy really ill—is there something more than I understand? Why didn't you tell me? Has their been an accident, perhaps? Why, I must go to him too—come—hurry—I'll go with you, of course."

Rex stumbled again in his effort to quiet her alarm, to prevent this scheme of seeking Billy on his couch of pain. "Oh no, indeed you mustn't do that," he objected strenuously. "I couldn't let you, you know. I don't want you to be bothered. Billy isn't ill at all—there hasn't been any accident, I give you my word. He's all right—Billy's all right." He had quite lost his prospective by now, and did not see the rocks upon which he rushed.

"If Billy's all right, why isn't he here?" demanded Billy's cousin severely.

Rex saw now. "He isn't exactly—that is to say—all right, you know. You see how it is," and he gazed involuntarily at the sleeping giant huddled on the truck.

"I do not see." The brown eyes had never looked at him so coldly before, and their expression cut him.

"I'm glad you don't," he cried, and realized that the words had taken him a step deeper into trouble. "It's just this way, Miss Margery—Billy isn't hurt or ill, but he isn't—isn't feeling quite himself, and—and I've got to—I've got to be with him." His voice sounded as if he were going to cry, but it moved the girl to no pity.

"Oh!" she said, and her bewildered tone was a whole world removed from the bright comradeship with which she had met him. "I see—you and Billy have something else planned." Her face flushed suddenly. "I'm sorry I misunderstood about—about the theater. I wouldn't for worlds have—have seemed to force you to—" She stopped, embarrassed, hurt, but yet with her graceful dignity untouched.

"Oh," the wretched Rex exclaimed impetuously, "if I could only take you to the theater, I'd rather than—" but the girl stopped him.

"Never mind about that, please," she said, with gentle decision. "I must go home—when is the next boat? One is going now—good-night, Mr. Fairfax —no, don't come with me—I don't need you," and she was gone.

Two minutes later Strong's innocent slumbers were dispersed by a vicious shake. "Wake up! wake up!" ordered Fairfax, restraining himself with difficulty from mangling the cause of his sufferings. "I've had enough, and we're going home, straight."

Rex was mistaken about that, but Billy was cordial in agreeing with him. "Good idea, Recky! Howd'y' ever come to think of it? Le's go home straight; tha's a bully good thing to do. Le's do it. Big head on you, ol' boy," and yawning still, but with unperturbed good nature, Strong marched, a bit crookedly, arm in arm with his friend to the street.

At every station the conductor and Rex had to reason with him

Rex's memory of the trip uptown on the Elevated was like an evil dream. Strong, after his nap, was as a giant refreshed, and his play of wit knew no contracting limits. There were, luckily, not many passengers going up at this hour, but the dozen or so on the car were regaled. Billy selected a seat on the floor with his broad back planted against the door, and at every station the conductor and Rex had to reason with him at length before the door could be opened. The official threatened as well as he could for laughing to put him off, but he threatened less strenuously for the sight of six feet two of muscle in magnificently fit condition. This lasted for half a dozen stations and then the patient began to play like a mountainous kitten. He took a strap on either side of the car and turned somersaults; he did traveling ring work with them; he gave a standing broad jump that would have been creditable on an athletic field; he had his audience screaming with laughter at an imitation of water polo over the back of a seat. Then, just as the fun was at an almost impossible point, and the conductor, highly entertained but worried, was considering how to get this chap arrested, Billy walked up to him with charming friendliness and shook hands.

"One th' besh track meets I've ever had pleasure attendin', sir," he said genially, and sat down and relapsed into grave dignity.

So he remained for five minutes, to the trembling joy of his exhausted guardian, but it was too good to be true. Suddenly, at Fifty-third Street, he spied a young woman at the other end of the car. There were not more than nine passengers, so that each person might have had a matter of half a dozen seats a piece, but Strong suddenly felt a demand on his politeness, and reason was nothing to him. He rose and marched the forty feet or so between himself and the woman, and, standing in front of her, lifted, with some difficulty, his hat.

"Won't you take my seat, madam?" he inquired, with a smile of perfect courtesy.

The young person was a young person of common-sense and she caught the situation. She flashed a reassuring glance at Rex, hovering distressed in the background, and shook her head at Strong politely. "No—no, thank you," she said; "I think I can find a seat at this end that will do nicely."

"Madam, I insist," Strong addressed her again earnestly.

"No, really," The young woman was embarrassed, for the eyes of the car were on her. "Thank you so much," she said finally; "I think I'd better stay here."

Strong bent over and put a great hand lightly on her arm. "Madam, as gen'leman I cannot, cannot allow it. Madam, you mush take my seat. Pleash, madam, do not make scene. 'S pleasure to me, 'sure you—greates' pleasure," and beneath this courtly urgency the flushed girl walked shamefacedly the length of the almost empty car, and sat down in Strong's seat, while that soul of chivalry put his hand through a strap and so stood till his ministering angel extracted him from the train at Seventy-second Street.

With a sigh of heartfelt relief, Rex put his arm in the big fellow's at the foot of the steps. Freedom must now be at hand, for Billy's home was in a great apartment building not ten minutes' walk away. The culprit himself seemed to realize that his fling was over.

"Raished Cain t'night, didn' we, ol' pal?" he inquired, and squeezed Rex's guiding arm with affection. "I'll shay this for you, Rex—you may be soft-hearted ol' slob, you may be half-witted donkey—I'm not denyin' all that 'n more, but I'll shay thish—you're the bes' man to go on a drunk with in—in —in The'logican Sem'nary. I'm not 'xceptin' th'——"

"Shut up, Billy," remarked Rex, not for the first time that night. "I'd get myself pulled together a bit if I were you," he advised. "You're going to see your family in a minute."

"M' poor fam'ly!" mourned Strong, shaking his head. "M' poor fam'ly! Thish'll be awful blow to m' fam'ly, Recky. They all like so mush to see me sober—always—'s their fad, Recky. Don't blame 'em, Recky, 's natural to 'em. Some peop' born that way. M' poor fam'ly."

They stood in front of the broad driveway which swept under lofty arches into the huge apartment house. Strong stopped and gazed upwards mournfully. "Right up there," he murmured, pointing skywards—"M' fam'ly." The tears were streaming down his face frankly now. "I can't face 'em Recky, 'n this condition you've got me in," he said more in sorrow than in anger. At that second the last inspiration of the evening caught him. Across the street arose the mighty pile of an enormous uptown hotel. Strong jerked his thumb over his shoulder. "Go'n' break it to m' fam'ly by telegraph' 'em," he stated, and bitterly Rex repented of that thoughtless mention of the Strongs to their son and heir.

Good-naturedly as he had done everything, but relentlessly, he dragged his victim over the way, and direct to the Western Union office of the hotel —"Webster's Union" he preferred to call it. His first telegram read:

"Rex Fairfax got me drunk. Don't blame him. It's natural to him."

That one was confiscated, Strong complaining gently that his friend was all "fads."

The second message was this:

"Dear Mama: Billy's intoxicated. Awfully sorry. Couldn't be helped. Home soon."

That one went in spite of Fairfax's efforts, with two cents extra to pay, which item was the first event of the evening to ruffle Strong's temper.

"Shame, shame on rich cap'talists like Webster's Union to wring two cents from poor drunk chap, for lil' word like 'soon'," he growled, and appealed to the operator. "Couldn't you let me off that two cents?" he asked winningly. "You're good fellow—good lookin' fellow too"—which was the truth. "Well, then, can I get 'em cheaper 'f I sen 'em by quantity? I'll do that—how many for dollar, hey?"

"Five," said the grinning operator, troubled by the irregularity, but taken by this highly entertaining scheme of telegraphing across the street. And Rex, his arts exhausted in vain, watched hopelessly while, one after another, five telegrams were sent to The Montana, a hundred feet away. The first being short two of the regulation ten words. Strong finished with a cabalistic phrase: "Rectangular parallelopipedon."

"That'll get even Webster's Union for chargin' me two cents for 'soon'," he chuckled. "Don't y' wish y' hadn' charged me that two cents, hey?" he demanded of the operator, laughing joyfully and cocking his hat over one ear, and the operator and two or three men who stood near could do no otherwise than laugh joyfully too. Strong straightened his face into a semblance of deep gravity. "Thish next one's important," he announced, and put the end of the pencil in his mouth and meditated, while his fascinated audience watched him. He was lost in thought for perhaps two minutes, and then scribbled madly, and as he ended the little bunch of men crowded frankly to look at what he had written. He pushed it toward them with charming unreserve, and the bewilderment with which it was read seemed to please him.

"Dear Papa": it ran. "I'm Calymene Blumembachii, a trilobite, one of the crustaceans related to the emtomostracans, but looking more like a tetradecapod, but always your affectionate—Billy."

He pushed it to the operator. "Split that in three," he ordered. "Don't want ruin the wires I'm careful 'bout wires. Big fall snow wouldn't do more damage 'n heavy words like that," he explained to the listening circle. "Think I look like tetradecapod?" he asked of them as one who makes conversation. "Had that in geology lesson when I was fifteen," he went on. "Got lodged in crack in brain and there tish t' thish day! Every now'n then I go 'flip,'"—he appeared to pull a light lever situated in his head—"'n fire it off. See? Always hit something."

It was ten o'clock when, the job lot of telegrams despatched, Fairfax led his volcano from the hotel and headed for the apartment house. He expected another balk at the entrance, for his round of gaiety had come now to seem to him eternal—he could hardly imagine a life in which he was not conducting a tipsy man through a maze of experiences. So that it was one of the surprises of the evening when Strong entered quietly and with perfect deportment took his place in the elevator and got out again, eight floors up, with the mildness of a dove. At the door of the apartment came the last brief but sharp action of the campaign.

"Recky," he said, taking Fairfax's shoulders in his great grasp, "no mother could be t' me what you've been."

"I hope not," Rex responded promptly, but Strong was not to be side-tracked.

"No mother 'n the world—not one—no sir!" he went on. His voice broke with feeling. "I'll nev' forget it—nev'—don't ask me to," he insisted. "Dear Recky—blessed old tomfool—I'm go'n kiss you good-night."

"You bet you're not," said Fairfax with emphasis. "Let go of me, you idiot," and he tried to loosen the hands on his shoulders.

But one of the most powerful men in New York had him in his grip, and Rex found himself suddenly folded in Billy's arms, while a chaste salute was planted full on his mouth. As he emerged a second later, disgusted and furious, from this tender embrace, the clang of the elevator twenty feet away caught his ear and, turning, his eyes met the astonished gaze of two young girls and their scornful, frowning father. At that moment the door of the Strongs' apartment opened, there was a vision of the elder Mr. Strong's distracted face, the yellow gleam of the last telegram in his hands, and Rex fled.

Two weeks later, a May breeze rustling through the greenness of the quadrangle, brushed softly the ivy-clad brick walls, and stole, like a runaway child to its playmate, through an open window of the Theological Seminary building at Chelsea Square. Entering so, it flapped suddenly at the white curtains as if astonished. What was this? Two muscular black clad arms were stretched across a table, and between them lay a brown head, inert, hopeless. It seemed strange that on such a May day, with such a May breeze, life could look dark to anything young, yet Reginald Fairfax, at the head of the graduating class, easily first in more than one way—in scholarship, in athletics, in versatility, and, more than all, like George Washington, "first in the hearts of his countrymen," the most popular man of the Seminary—this successful and well beloved young person sat wretched and restless in his room and let the breeze blow over his prostrate head and his idle, nerveless hands. Since the night of the rescue of Billy Strong he had felt himself another and a worse man. He sent a note to his cousin the next day.

"Dear Carty," it read, "For mercy sake let me alone. I know I've lost my chance at St. Eric's and I know you'll say it was my own fault. I don't want to hear either statement, so don't come near me till I hunt you up, which I will do when I'm fit to talk to a white man. I'm grateful, though you may not believe it. Yours—Rex."

But the lost chance at St. Eric's, although it was coming to weigh heavily on his buoyant spirit, was not the worst of his troubles. The girl from Orange— there lay the sting. He had sent her a note as well, but there was little he was free to say without betraying Billy, the note was mostly vague expressions of regret, and Rex knew her clearheaded directness too well to hope that it would count for much. No answer had come, and, day by day, he had grown more dejected, hoping against hope for one.

A knock—the postman's knock—and Rex started and sprang to the door. One letter, but he could hardly believe his glad eyes when he saw the address on it, for it was the handwriting which he had come to know well, had known well, seeing it once—her handwriting. In a moment the jagged-edged envelope, torn in a desperate hurry to get what it held, lay one side, and he was reading.

"Dear Mr. Fairfax": the letter ran; "For two weeks I have been very unjust to you and I want to beg your pardon. Billy was here three days ago, and what I didn't know and what he didn't know we patched together, and the consequence is I want to apologize and to make up to you, if I can, for being so disagreeable. Billy's recollections of that night were disjointed, but he remembered a lot in spots, and I know now just what a friend you were to him and how you saved him. I think he was horrid, but I think you were fine—simply fine. I can't half say it in writing so will you please come out for over Sunday—mother says—and I'll try to show you how splendid I think you were. Will you? Yours sincerely"—and her name.

Would he? Such a radiant smile shone through the little bare room that the May breeze, catching its light at the window, clapped gay applause against the flapping curtain. This was as it should be.

But the breeze and the postman were not to be the only messengers of happiness. Steps sounded down the long, empty hall, stopped at his door, and Rex, a new joy of living pulsing through him, sprang again, almost before the knock sounded, to meet gladly what might be coming. His face looked out of the wide-open doorway with so bright a welcome to the world, that the two men who stood across the threshold smiled an involuntary answer.

"Carty! I'm awfully glad"—and Rex stopped to put his hand out graciously, deferentially, to the gray-haired and distinguished man who stood with Carter Reed.

"Judge Rush, this is my cousin, Mr. Fairfax," Reed presented him, and in a moment Rex's friend, the breeze, was helping hospitality on with gay little refreshing dashes at a warm, silvered head, as Judge Rush sat in the biggest chair at the big open window. He beamed upon the young man with interested, friendly eyes.

"That's all very well about the quadrangle, Mr. Reed. It certainly is beautiful and like the English Universities," he broke into a sentence genially. "But I wish to talk to Mr. Fairfax. I've come to bring you the first news, Mr. Fairfax, of what you will hear officially within a day or two—that the vestry of St. Eric's hope you will consider a call to be our assistant rector." Rex's heart almost stopped beating, and his smile faded as he stared breathless at this portly and beneficent Mercury. Mercury went on "A vestry meeting was held last night in which this was decided upon. Your brilliant record in this seminary and other qualifications which have been mentioned to us by high authorities, were the reasons for this action which appeared upon the surface, but I want you to know the inner workings—I asked your cousin to bring me here that I might have the pleasure of telling you."

It was rather warm, and the old gentleman had climbed stairs, and his conversation had been weighty and steady. He arrested its flow for a moment and took a long breath. "Don't stop," said Rex earnestly, and the others broke into sudden laughter.

"I like that," Judge Rush sputtered, chuckling. "You're ready to let me kill myself, if needs be, to get the facts. All right, young man—I like impetuosity—it means energy. I'll go on. The facts not known to the public, which I wish to tell you, are as follows. After your failure to keep your appointment on the evening of the 7th, I was about through with you. I considered you careless both of your own interests and ours, and we began to look for another assistant. A man who fitted the place as you did seemed hard to find and the case was *in statu quo* when, two nights ago, my son brought home young William Strong to dinner. Our families are old friends and Billy's father and I were chums in college, so the boy is at home in our house. As you probably know, he has the gift of telling a good story, so when he began on the events of an evening which you will remember——"

Rex's deep laughter broke into the dignified sentences at this point.

"I see you remember." Judge Rush smiled benignly. "Well, Mr. Fairfax, Billy made an amusing story of that evening. Only the family were at the table and he spared himself not at all. He had been in Orange the day before, and the young lady in the case had told him how you had protected him at your own expense—he made that funny too, but I thought it very fine behavior—very fine, indeed, sir." Rex's face flushed under this. "And as I thought the whole affair over afterwards, I not only understood why you had failed me, but I honored you for attempting no explanation, and I made up my mind that you were the man we wanted. Yes, sir, the man we want. A man who knows how to deal with the situations of to-day, with the vices of a great city, that is what we want. I consider tact, and broadmindedness and self-sacrifice no small qualities for a minister of the gospel; and a combination of those qualities, as in you, I consider exceptional. So I went to this vestry meeting primed, and I told them we had got to have you, sir—and we've got to. You'll come?"

The question was much like an order, but Rex did not mind. "Indeed, I'll come, Judge Rush," he said, and his manner of saying it won the last doubtful bit of the Judge's heart.

The Sunday morning when the new assistant preached his first sermon in St. Eric's, there sat well back in the congregation a dark-eyed girl, and with her a tall and powerful young man, whose deep shoulders and movements, as of a well fitted machine, advertised an athlete in perfect form. The girl's face was rapt as she followed, her soul in her eyes, the clean-cut, short sermon, and when the congregation filtered slowly down the aisles she said not a word. But as the two turned into the street she spoke at last.

"He is a saint, isn't he, Billy?" she asked, and drew a long breath of contentment.

And from six-feet-two in mid-air came Billy Strong's dictum. "Margery," he said, impressively, "Rex may be a parson and all that, but, to my mind, that's not against him; to my mind that suits his style of handling the gloves. There was a chap in the Bible"—Billy swallowed as if embarrassed—"who —who was the spit 'n' image of Rex—the good Samaritan chap, you know. He found a seedy one falling over himself by the wayside, and he called him a beast and set him up, and took him to a hotel or something and told the innkeeper to charge it to him, and—I forget the exact words, but he saw him through, don't you know? And he did it all in a sporty sort of way and there wasn't a word of whining or fussing at him because he was loaded— that was awfully white of the chap. Rex did more than that for me and not a syllable has he peeped since. And, you know, the consequence of that masterly silence is that I've gone on the water-wagon—yes, sir—for a year. And I'm hanged if I'm not going to church every Sunday. He may be a saint as you say, and I suppose there's no doubt but he's horrid intellectual— every man must have his weaknesses. But the man that's a good Samaritan and a good sport all in one, he's my sort, I'm for him," said Billy Strong.